MR. JENSEN & CAT

Lenore Blegvad

Mr. Jensen & Cat

ILLUSTRATED BY ERIK BLEGVAD

HARCOURT, BRACE & WORLD, INC., NEW YORK

For my families

Although Mr. Jensen had a cat, he was lonely. They lived together in the big city of Copenhagen, which Mr. Jensen loved more than any other place in Denmark. But even so, and even though the cat kept him good company, he was lonely.

Sometimes he thought perhaps he ought to have a wife.

"That would be nice," he would say to his cat. "We'd have someone to talk to." He could almost imagine how she would look. She would be a smiling sort of person. Her hair would be tied back in a nice bun. She would wear a pink checked apron around her waist when she was in the kitchen.

"But I can't marry someone I don't even know," he would decide. And then he would go on living the way he always had. And feeling just as lonely.

He was lonely, for example, on weekdays—on *Mandag* (which is Monday in Danish), on *Tirsdag* (which is Tuesday), on *Onsdag* (Wednesday), *Torsdag* (Thursday), *Fredag* (Friday), and *Lørdag* (Saturday).

On those days Mr. Jensen went to work. Oh, he did not mind working. In fact, he loved it. You see, Mr. Jensen was a toymaker. And that is a nice thing to be. He made Danish fishing boats and Danish soldiers and Danish farm animals out of wood and painted them in cheerful colors. But in the sunny room where he sat and worked, he was all alone. The shopkeeper stayed in the next room to take care of the customers, and Mr. Jensen was left with no one to talk to at all.

Even riding back and forth to work on his bicycle, there was no one to talk to. All the hundreds of people bicycling near to him were busy, tinkling their bicycle bells, watching the traffic, signaling directions. They were far too busy to stop and talk.

So Mr. Jensen's weekdays were lonely. Unfortunately, each *Søndag* (Sunday) was even more so. Yet on Sundays he did the things he liked the best.

Some Sundays he walked by the canals to watch the fishing boats unload their catch. On others he went to the cobblestone square in front of the King's palace to watch the changing of the guard. There were some Sundays that he spent climbing the tall towers of Copenhagen to see the views. On Sundays in the summertime, especially at night when it never really gets quite dark, he went to the Tivoli Gardens to see the colored lights and to have a ride on the Ferris wheel.

Many people everywhere in Copenhagen knew Mr. Jensen by sight. Some even knew him by name. The fisherman and some of the soldiers on the palace square would say, *"God dag, Herr Jensen,"* (Good day, Mr. Jensen) when they saw him. They liked his quick step and his hair that never seemed combed and the scarf he wound around his neck in the winter.

Then why was Mr. Jensen so lonely? Because he was shy. He was so shy that he could just nod his head in reply whenever someone said, *"God dag, Herr Jensen."*

So Sundays were nice. But they were lonesome, too.

And that is why, at home, Mr. Jensen had a cat. To keep him company.

One *Tirsdag* morning the cat, as usual, jumped up on Mr. Jensen's big feather quilt to wake him up. Mr. Jensen heard the wind rattling the hooks on the window.

"A cold, blowy day," he told his cat. "I must remember to wear my scarf." The cat curled up in the quilt and

11

began to wash its paws. Mr. Jensen went to the back door to fetch the rolls and the milk the dairy boy brought each morning. But this morning there was nothing on the door mat.

"Strange," Mr. Jensen said. "That's the first time he hasn't come. I hope he hasn't caught cold. Very strange." He poured a dish of yesterday's milk for the cat. Then he made a pot of tea for himself and covered it with the cozy. He liked to have his breakfast at the little table in front of the window. There he could look out on the red rooftops of Copenhagen. The cat came and curled up among the flowerpots on the windowsill. It always lay there at breakfast time and watched the sea gulls swoop past. The sea gulls were very active this morning, riding on the wind or hanging almost motionless in the air. But for once, the cat did not seem very interested.

"Strange," Mr. Jensen said again. "What is the matter with everyone this morning?" The cat even got up and went back to the quilt. When Mr. Jensen was ready to leave for work, it did not come to the door with him as it usually did.

"Well then, *missekat*," (pussycat) Mr. Jensen called as he went out the door. *"Farvel, farvel,"* (Good-by, good-by). And off he went to fetch his bicycle from the courtyard.

But to his surprise, it had a flat tire. He tried to pump it up, but he knew it wouldn't help. It was that kind of day. Very odd.

"I shall go by trolley," Mr. Jensen decided. "I haven't done that in a long time."

As he came out of the house, a sweeping gust of wind tried to blow him over! It tried so hard that it almost made him slam the door in the face of a lady who came running down the stairs behind him. The lady smiled at him and said it didn't matter. Mr. Jensen apologized and ran for his trolley.

Finally he arrived at the toy shop. As he opened the door, he could hear the telephone ringing. He ran for that, too. It was the shopkeeper.

"I won't be coming in today," he announced to Mr. Jensen. That had never happened before. "I have had an accident."

15

"What has happened?" cried Mr. Jensen.

"A pretzel has fallen on my toe!" the shopkeeper said.

"A pretzel?" Mr. Jensen was amazed. "How can a pretzel cause an accident?"

The shopkeeper tried to explain. "Not a real pretzel, Herr Jensen. One of those tremendous gold ones made out of wood that hang outside the bakery shops. The wind blew it down."

"You mean a baker's sign? It fell on your toe?" Mr. Jensen knew that would be very painful.

"Yes, yes, and I can't walk," the shopkeeper said. "So I must ask you to do me a favor and deliver a dozen soldiers to one of the customers in your lunch hour." Mr. Jensen said he would be glad to. What a strange day! A day full of surprises.

There were even more surprises at lunch hour. Every day Mr. Jensen brought a little package of black bread sandwiches from home to the toy shop. All Danes eat little black bread sandwiches for lunch. Mr. Jensen ate his as usual. Then he started out to deliver the soldiers. He wound his scarf around his neck. He tucked the large cardboard box under one arm. He set off toward the Town Hall Square.

Near the King's palace he passed along the edge of a busy canal. It was very windy. All at once the wind blew the cover of the box loose. It blew and blew against the cover, pushing inside it like a sail, and before he knew it, the whole box of soldiers was blown out of Mr. Jensen's arms into the canal!

18

The box sank immediately, but the soldiers, being made of wood, bobbed one by one up to the surface of the water. Everybody in the street stopped to watch. A tourist boat passing through the canal stopped, too, full of curious sightseers.

19

A sailor coming out of a shop jumped into a rowboat that was tied up at the edge of the canal. He rowed out to the little fleet of soldiers who were floating, some on their stomachs peering down into the water, some on their backs staring up at the sky, and fished them all out.

"Hooray!" cheered some children who were watching. Mr. Jensen thanked the sailor, who put the soldiers in a neat row on the edge of the canal.

"Well, now," Mr. Jensen said to the children. "I don't think I can deliver salt-water-soaked soldiers to my customer, do you? I will give them to you instead." He handed them out to the children. There was one soldier left over. Mr. Jensen gave it to the sailor.

"Oh, *tak, tak*," (thank you, thank you) the children said, delighted.

"*Tusind tak*," (A thousand thanks) the sailor said and saluted. Mr. Jensen nodded his head and went back to the shop to fetch another box of soldiers for the customer.

That evening in the trolley on the way home, Mr. Jensen saw the lady he had nearly shut in the door that morning. She smiled at him, and they walked together from the trolley toward their house. On the way she stopped to buy a bunch of flowers at the florist.

"I miss my garden in the country," she explained. "I have just moved to Copenhagen, you see. That is, my cats and I. I have three cats."

"I have a cat, too," Mr. Jensen said quite bravely. "I was just going to buy some fish for his dinner." The fishmonger's shop was next to the florist. The lady came into the shop with Mr. Jensen. She helped him choose a fish from the tiled tank. Then she chose two for herself, and the fishmonger fished them all out of the tank with a little net.

When they got to the house, the lady said *farvel* as they reached the second floor. She smiled again, and Mr. Jensen made a little bow. Then he continued on up the stairs to the top floor. He knew his cat would be waiting for him just inside the door. But it wasn't. Mr. Jensen could see it still curled up on his quilt. He did not want to waken it, but he was sorry the cat was sleeping. He wished he had someone to tell about this very strange and unusual day. Even his cat would be better than no one at all.

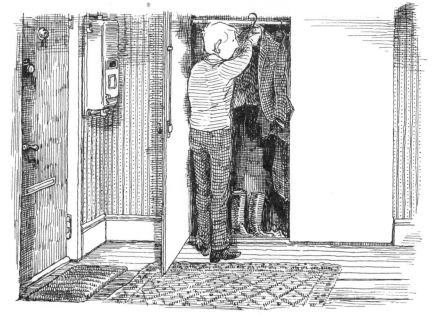

Mr. Jensen began to feel quite sorry for himself. He didn't even feel like cooking his dinner, although there was a lovely plateful of meat patties quite ready to fry. He looked in the bedroom at the cat.

"What good are you?" he said to it in such an un-friendly way that he even surprised himself. "You're not much of a companion, I must say."

Suddenly the cat looked up at him, and Mr. Jensen could see at once that it was sick. He rushed and picked it up in his arms. The cat was very limp, and its nose was hot and dry. Mr. Jensen did not know what to do. He tried to give it some warm milk, but it did not even open its eyes to look at the saucer. What could be the matter? Mr. Jensen did not want to take the cat out in the cold wind to the veterinarian. What should he do?

Then he remembered the lady on the second floor who had three cats. She would know what to do. Mr. Jensen forgot all about feeling sorry for himself. He wrapped the cat in his warmest tweed jacket and went quickly down the stairs to the second floor.

"Who is there?" the lady called when Mr. Jensen rang the bell.

"Herr Jensen," Mr. Jensen said. "From the top floor. Herr Jensen and *kat*."

The lady was not at all surprised to see him. She understood at once why he had come. Her three cats walked all around Mr. Jensen's feet while he stood and watched their mistress.

She took a little pill out of an envelope and opened the jaws of the sick cat. Quickly she popped the pill into its mouth. Then she massaged its throat to make sure the pill went down. She gave the cat some water in a little dish, and it lapped up a tiny bit with its tongue.

"Just a little fever," the lady explained. "My cats all had it last week. That's why I have these pills. Tomorrow everything will be all right." The cat had gone to sleep again on Mr. Jensen's coat.

Mr. Jensen himself felt quite weak with relief.

"*Tusind tak*," he said. Then he had to sit down. At once all three of the lady's cats jumped into his lap. And then another strange thing happened. Mr. Jensen's own cat raised its head and looked at all those cats lying in a pile on Mr. Jensen's lap. Then it slowly got up and jumped into the middle of the pile. There was a wild confusion of fur and paws! Mr. Jensen seemed completely covered with cats. But just as suddenly, it was over. The cats all settled down on Mr. Jensen's lap, one by one, and began to purr. All four of them.

The lady laughed. Mr. Jensen laughed, too, but carefully so as not to disturb the cats.

"You must stay and have dinner with us," the lady said. "Now that we are all such good friends."

Mr. Jensen was delighted. He decided that during dinner he would talk about his lovely city of Copenhagen and the most interesting things to see there. But all at

once he noticed something *so* strange, *so* odd, so *really* unusual that he changed his mind. He had noticed, as the lady went into the kitchen, that her hair was pinned up in a nice bun in the back! He had noticed that the apron she was tying around her waist had a pattern of pink checks!

31

Hadn't he wished for someone he could tell about the day he had just spent? Now his wish had come true. Mr. Jensen decided to tell the lady all about this day. The most extraordinary day he had ever had.

And the nicest!